D0459487

MARC BROWN

ARTHUR'S HALLOWEEN

Little, Brown and Company • Hachette Book Group • 237 Park Avenue, New York, NY 10017 • Visit our website at www.lb-kids.com

Little, Brown and Company is a division of Hachette Book Group, Inc. • The Little, Brown name and logo are trademarks of Hachette Book Group, Inc.

The publisher is not responsible for websites (or their content) that are not owned by the publisher.

First Revised Edition: August 2011 • First published in hardcover in September 1982 by Little, Brown and Company
Arthur® is a registered trademark of Marc Brown.

Library of Congress Cataloging-in-Publication Data
Brown, Marc Tolon.
Arthur's Halloween / Marc Brown.—1st ed. p. cm.
Summary: Arthur finds everything about Halloween scary, including his little sister's costume, his morning snack, and the big house on the corner.
ISBN 978-0-316-11116-4 (hc) / ISBN 978-0-316-11059-4 (pb)
[1. Halloween—Fiction.] I. Title
P27.B81618Aq [E] — dc20   82-15286

40 39 38 37 36 35 34 33 32 31
SC • Printed in China

LITTLE, BROWN AND COMPANY
New York   Boston

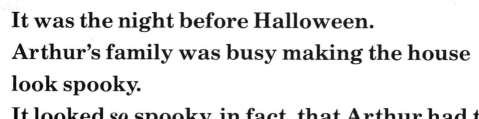

It was the night before Halloween.
Arthur's family was busy making the house
look spooky.
It looked *so* spooky, in fact, that Arthur had trouble
falling asleep.

Things were even worse the next morning.
"Help!" screamed Arthur when he opened his eyes.
"It's just me," said his sister, D.W.
"Boy, are you jumpy. Don't forget,
you have to take me trick-or-treating tonight."

"Do I really have to?" asked Arthur
as he ate his cereal.
"You really do," said his mother.
"And, I want to go to *every* house," said D.W.
Arthur groaned. "I'll be the only one who has to
drag his baby sister along."

Arthur didn't recognize anyone at school.
There was a giant robot in his classroom
taking attendance.

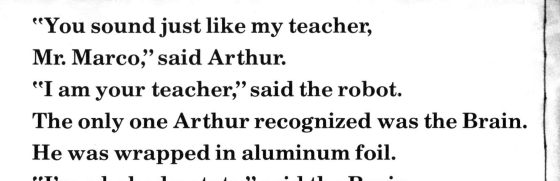

"You sound just like my teacher,
Mr. Marco," said Arthur.
"I am your teacher," said the robot.
The only one Arthur recognized was the Brain.
He was wrapped in aluminum foil.
"I'm a baked potato," said the Brain.

Francine passed out special morning snacks.
"Eat these," she said. "They're bat-wing brownies
and vampire blood."
Everyone ate them but Arthur.

Then they all put on blindfolds.
Buster passed around bowls he said were filled
with human eyeballs, hearts and brains.
Arthur turned pale.
When it was his turn, he wouldn't even touch them.
"What a scaredy-cat," said Francine.
"Chicken!" said Muffy.
"They're only peeled grapes, Jell-O
and cold spaghetti."

When it came time to go trick-or-treating
Buster knew which houses to skip.
"Don't go there," he said. "They only give apples."
"Gross," said Francine.

"And don't go to the big house on the corner," said Buster. "That's the witch's house." "My brother saw someone go in there last Halloween and he never came out." Arthur tried not to look afraid.

Arthur and his sister had trouble keeping up
with the others.
First D.W. got her tail caught.
Then her bag broke.
"You're such a pain in the neck," said Arthur.
"D.W. must be short for Dim Wit."
But D.W. didn't answer.
Arthur turned around just in time to see her
disappear into the witch's house.

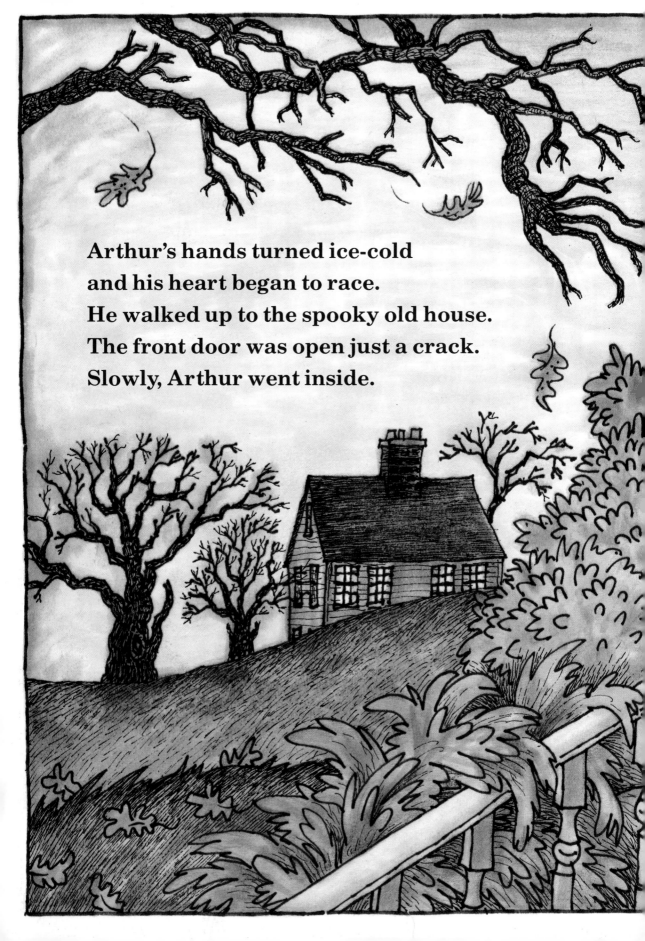

Arthur's hands turned ice-cold
and his heart began to race.
He walked up to the spooky old house.
The front door was open just a crack.
Slowly, Arthur went inside.

"Look," cried Buster. "Arthur just went into the witch's house!"

"She'll probably put Arthur and D.W. into
her oven, just like Hansel and Gretel,"
said Sue Ellen.
"Maybe she's using them for weird scientific
experiments," said the Brain.
"I bet she locked them in the cellar
to starve," said Buster.
"Maybe we should follow him," said Francine.
"Maybe we should call the police," said Muffy.
Everyone was too scared to move.

Inside the house it was very cold.

Arthur thought he saw ghosts all around him.

He walked down a long dark hall.

At the end he saw a light under a door.

He heard voices.

One was his sister's.

"Oh, there you are," said the witch.
"We were waiting for you."
"I came to get my sister. We have to go.
I hear my mother calling us," said Arthur.
"I don't hear anything," said D.W.
"My name is Mrs. Tibble. I hope you won't leave
without some cider and doughnuts first."
"They're chocolate. Your favorite," said D.W.

"I've waited all night for trick-or-treaters,
but you're the only ones," said Mrs. Tibble.
"Years ago our doorbell never stopped ringing."
"Maybe it's broken like the windows," said D.W.

Mrs. Tibble nodded. "It is harder for me to keep
up with this big place these days."
"Maybe if we help you fix up your yard,
the place won't look so spooky," said Arthur.

Arthur finished his doughnut as Mrs. Tibble
opened the door and turned on the porch light.
She gave Arthur and D.W. a big hug.
"See you Saturday to rake leaves," said Arthur.

"You're still alive!" said Francine.
"I can't believe you went in there alone,"
said the Brain.
"You're so brave," said Sue Ellen.
"What's in the bag?" asked Buster.
"Probably eyeballs, hearts and brains!"
said Francine.

"It's easy to find out," said Arthur. "Just close
your eyes and reach in unless you're too scared."
"We've been to every house now. Can we take
the shortcut home through the cemetery?" asked D.W.
"The cemetery! On Halloween!
Are you guys crazy?" asked Francine.